Mount
Tale
of
Norway

Contents

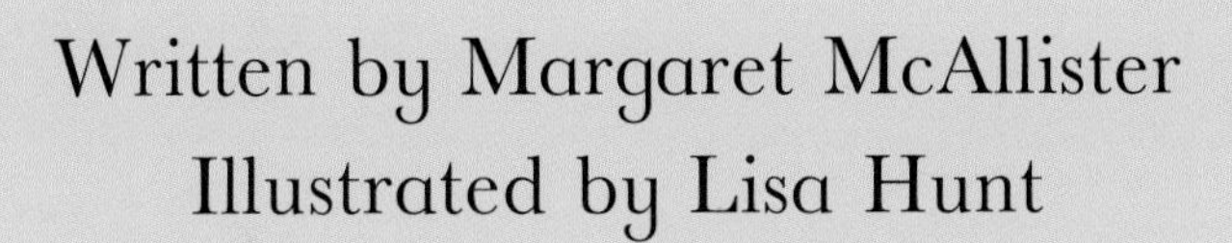
Written by Margaret McAllister
Illustrated by Lisa Hunt

Published by Pearson Education Limited, Edinburgh Gate, Harlow, Essex, CM20 2JE.

www.pearsonschools.co.uk

Designed by Bigtop

Illustrated by Lisa Hunt, The Organisation

First published 2013

17 16
10 9 8 7 6 5 4
British Library Cataloguing in Publication Data
A catalogue record for this book is available from the British Library

ISBN 978 0 435 14371 8

Printed and bound by Golden Cup (GCC/04)

Acknowledgements
We would like to thank Bangor Central Integrated Primary School, Northern Ireland; Bishop Henderson Church of England Primary School, Somerset; Bletchingdon Parochial Church of England Primary School, Oxfordshire; Brookside Community Primary School, Somerset; Bude Park Primary School, Hull; Cheddington Combined School, Buckinghamshire; Dair House Independent School, Buckinghamshire; Deal Parochial School, Kent; Glebe Infant School, Gloucestershire; Henley Green Primary School, Coventry; Lovelace Primary School, Surrey; Our Lady of Peace Junior School, Slough; Tackley Church of England Primary School, Oxfordshire; and Twyford Church of England School, Buckinghamshire for their invaluable help in the development and trialling of the Bug Club resources.

Every effort has been made to contact copyright holders of material reproduced in this book. Any omissions will be rectified in subsequent printings if notice is given to the publishers.

The Happiest People of the Hills

Based on a Norwegian folk story collected by Asbjørnsen and Moe

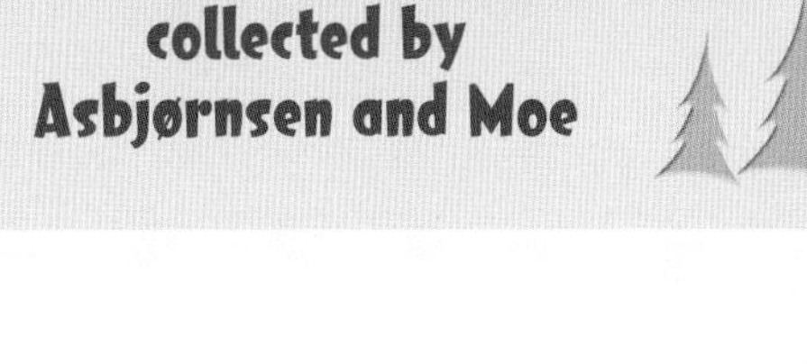

Chapter 1
Gudbrand and Marit

The steep hills of Norway are green with lush meadows and forests, and dotted with wooden houses. At the bottom of the hills runs the long, clear blue water of the fjords. Gudbrand and his wife, Marit, lived in a farmhouse above a fjord and were very happy – perhaps the happiest people on the hills.

They never, ever, quarrelled. Every morning, Gudbrand took their two cows up to the meadow to eat the best grass, and every evening, he brought them down again for milking.

One evening, Marit said to him, "Do we need both of those cows? We don't need that much milk. If we sell one we'll have some pocket money to spend, and that would be useful. You might get forty silver pieces or more for her. What do you think?"

Gudbrand thought this was a very good idea.

Chapter 2
The Long Walk

Early one summer's morning, Gudbrand took a cow on the long walk – and it was a *very* long walk – down to the town and into the market place. Unfortunately, nobody wanted to buy a cow.

When the market closed, Gudbrand set out to walk home – and it was *such* a long walk – back to the farmhouse high in the mountains.

He hadn't gone far when he met a young woman with a horse.

"That's a fine cow!" said the woman. "Just the sort of cow I want!"

"That's a fine horse!" said Gudbrand, thinking that a horse would be useful. So he traded the cow for the horse and went on his way.

Further along the road, he met a man with a goat. A goat, he thought, would be much more useful than a horse. Horses are expensive to feed, after all.

He and Marit could get milk, butter and cheese from a goat, and he could put the animal on the roof to keep the grass short! He did a deal with the man and swapped the horse for the goat.

The trouble with goats, though, he thought as he walked along, is that they eat everything – so when he met a man with a sheep, he was happy to exchange the goat for the sheep.

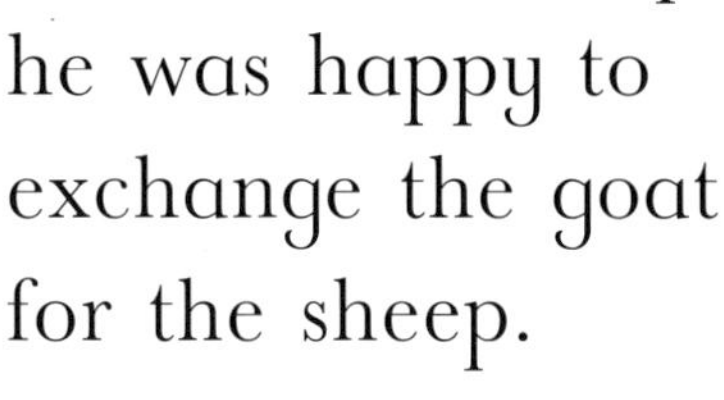

He continued on his way, with the sheep bleating and stopping to munch grass now and again.

The next person he met was a woman carrying a goose. Gudbrand thought that a goose feather bed would be very comfortable for him and Marit, so he swapped the sheep for the goose.

Along he went with the goose under his arm, but it was a noisy, heavy goose that hissed, wriggled and tried to bite him.

Then he met a man with a cockerel. He was very glad to swap the goose for the cockerel. A cockerel would be much easier to manage than a goose.

By now, Gudbrand had been walking for hours and hours.

"I'm still miles from home," he thought, "and I'm so hungry I feel weak. If I don't eat soon, I might starve to death, here in the road!"

Chapter 3
"Oh Yes, She Will!"

Gudbrand plodded on slowly, feeling hungrier and hungrier with every step, until he came to an inn where the smell of food was so delicious that he felt faint with hunger. He went in, swapped the cockerel for a good hot dinner, then, feeling much better, he went on his way.

He was nearly home when he met one of his neighbours.

"How did you do at the market?" asked his neighbour. When Gudbrand explained how he had started with a cow and ended with nothing, his neighbour was shocked.

"What will Marit say when you get home?" he asked. "She'll be furious!"

Gudbrand smiled at him. "She won't," he said. "She never is!"

"She will be this time!" laughed Gudbrand's neighbour.

"I say she won't!" said Gudbrand.

"Oh yes, she will!" insisted his neighbour. "Look, I'll make a deal with you. I'll go and stand outside your window and listen while you tell her what you did. If she isn't angry, I'll pay you a hundred silver pieces."

"Done!" said Gudbrand, shaking his neighbour's hand. "You can hide at the back window!"

Chapter 4
What Will She Say?

When Gudbrand reached home, his neighbour hurried round the house and hid at the back window to listen.

"My dear!" cried Marit as he came in through the door, "I'm so glad you're home safely! What happened at the market?"

"Nobody wanted to buy the cow," said Gudbrand. "But I traded her for a horse."

“A horse to ride!” she exclaimed. “Well done! I’ll feel such a grand lady, riding to visit my friends!”

“But then I traded the horse for a goat,” he continued.

“And a good thing too!” said Marit. “What use is a horse? They cost so much to keep. A goat will keep the grass short on the roof, and we can have milk.”

“No, we can’t,” said Gudbrand, “because I traded the goat for a sheep.”

"Quite right too," said Marit. "Goats are noisy and smelly. They eat all the flowers in the garden and the washing on the line, too. Sheep are much less trouble than goats, and I can spin the fleece into good warm wool."

"But then I met a woman, and I traded the sheep for a goose," Gudbrand went on.

"Perfect!" exclaimed Marit. "I hate spinning! Now we can have a lovely goose feather bed!"

"I'm afraid not," he told her. "I traded the goose for a cockerel."

"A cockerel!" she said. "That's exactly what we need! An alarm clock!"

"But then," he admitted, "I was so hungry, my dear, so very hungry, I thought I would die of starvation there on the road. What could I do? I traded the cockerel for a dinner. So, you see, I returned home to you with nothing."

Marit threw her arms around her husband and hugged him tightly.

"You brought yourself home, and that's all I want!" she said. "You might have died on the road, and what would I do without you? As long as I have you, I don't want anything else!"

Gudbrand's neighbour had never been so astonished in his life and paid him the hundred silver pieces, just as he had said. So at the end of a bad day's trading, Gudbrand and Marit had one cow, one hundred silver pieces, and each other. Were they the happiest people on the mountain?

I should think so.

Troll Trouble

Based on a Norwegian folk story
collected by
Asbjørnsen and Moe

Chapter 1
Halvor's Problem

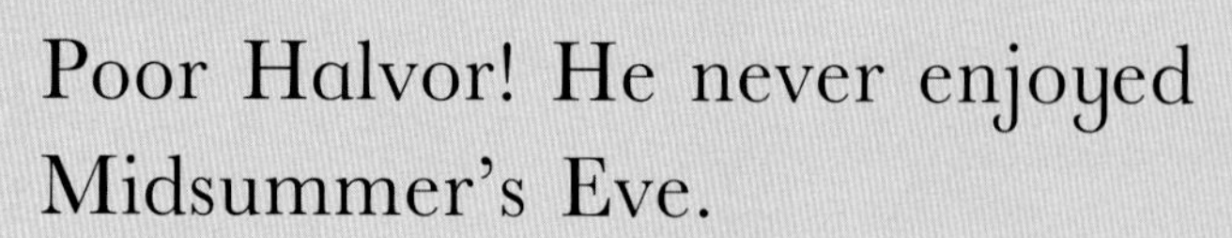

Poor Halvor! He never enjoyed Midsummer's Eve.

Halvor lived in Norway where the midsummer days are long and warm. Cows graze all day on the pastures, flowers grow in the meadows, and sunlight sparkles on the water. The sun stays up late, and so do the people. On Midsummer's Eve there are parties and bonfires.

So why didn't Halvor enjoy it? He enjoyed his work as a woodcutter, and he was happy in his wooden house in the mountains, but trolls lived in the mountains too. Some were as big as boulders and some were small and round, some had tails, most were ugly, and all of them were horrid.

Every Midsummer's Eve whole families of trolls would swarm down the mountain, stamping, singing and laughing all the way to Halvor's door.

And why did they pick on Halvor? Because his house was the nearest – that was all!

They would force the door open and push their way into the house, knocking over whatever was in their way.

They liked to sing loudly and dance wildly, bumping into the furniture …

… so that plates, cups and saucers fell from their shelves and smashed on the floor.

Most of all, they liked to eat. They'd eat all the food they could find, and drink all the drinks …

… and climb up the curtains so they could swing from the beams in the ceiling.

Finally, they would break a few more dishes just for fun and stamp away home up the hill.

Halvor never stayed at home on Midsummer's Eve. There was nothing he could do to get rid of the troublesome trolls, so every year he packed some things and went to stay with his brother.

There came one Midsummer's Eve when the sun was not shining at all. Lightning flashed, thunder roared, and rain poured down from the sky. As Halvor sheltered in his little wooden house, packing his things to take to his brother's, there was a knock at the door.

It couldn't be the trolls. Trolls never knocked! Halvor went to answer it.

A tall man with a pleasant look about him stood outside in the thunderstorm. Beside him, on all fours, was a large brown bear. The bear was enormous, and its claws looked sharp and strong. Halvor wondered what its teeth were like.

“Good afternoon!” said the man, pulling his coat around him against the rain. “My name is Rolf, and I’m sorry to trouble you, but I’m on my way to see the king. I’m taking him this fine brown bear as a present, but I’ve been caught in the storm. May I shelter here? Don’t worry about the bear. She’s as good as gold, as long as you don’t annoy her.”

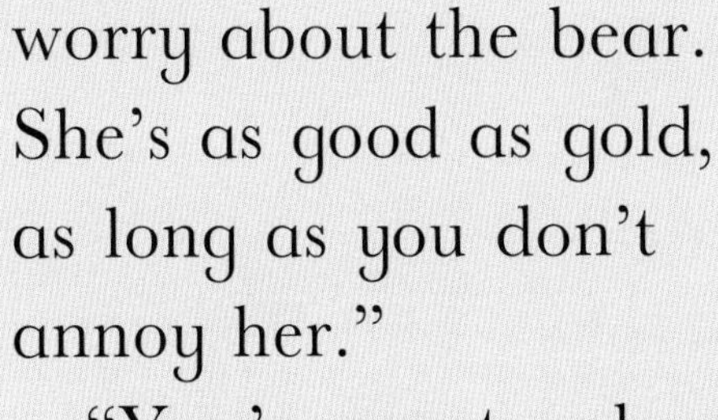

“You’re most welcome,” said Halvor, but he watched the bear nervously and didn’t get close to it.

He welcomed the stranger in and spread the man’s wet coat in front of the stove to dry.

"But you'd better not be here at nightfall. Not even I stay here late on Midsummer's Eve, when the trolls come down the mountain." And he told Rolf all about the trolls.

"In that case," said Rolf, "I really should stay here tonight, so you won't be alone when the trolls come. The bear will sleep under the table and be no bother at all."

So Halvor and Rolf stayed in the house. They ate supper together and gave the bear some fish. She enjoyed it very much and then fell asleep under the table, just as Rolf had said.

Chapter 3
Tramp, Tramp, Tramp

As night fell, they heard the tramp, tramp, tramp of troll feet stamping their way down the mountain.

"Here they come!" said Halvor anxiously.

"Let them come!" said Rolf. "I think we should step outside, hide by the window at the back of the house and watch what happens."

So that is what they did, although Halvor didn't really want to watch what the trolls would do to his house.

In came the trolls, pushing through the door. Stamp, went the huge hairy feet of the big rough trolls. Swish, went their tails across the floor, and the little ones screamed with laughter as they climbed the curtains. They all hunted through the cupboards and helped themselves. They gobbled down the bread and cooked all the fish they could find.

They gulped down the milk so greedily that they spilled half of it on the floor. The small trolls chased each other round and round the table, and one of them thought it would be fun to hide underneath it. He lifted the cloth and wriggled underneath.

Oh? What is that? he wondered. It was dark under there, and he could feel something furry. *It must be Halvor's cat!* he thought to himself. The little troll wanted to have some fun teasing her. He grabbed a fork from the table, stuck it into a sizzling hot piece of fish, and then tugged the bear's ear.

"Kitty!" he said, waving the fork under its nose. "Kitty want some fish?"

The bear didn't wake up, so the little troll pulled its ear hard and repeated, "Kitty want some fish?"

Slowly, the bear opened her eyes. Very softly, she growled. Then she opened her mouth wider and wider, showed her strong sharp teeth and suddenly sprang! Snarling and roaring she leapt from under the table and chased the trolls around and around.

All the trolls picked up their tails and ran. They were so terrified that they fell over each other as they stumbled out of the door. Some of them climbed the chimney to escape and rolled out at the top. Soon there wasn't a troll left in the house. The bear turned herself slowly round and went back to sleep under the table.

Rolf and Halvor watched from the back window.

"I don't think you'll have trouble with them again," said Rolf.